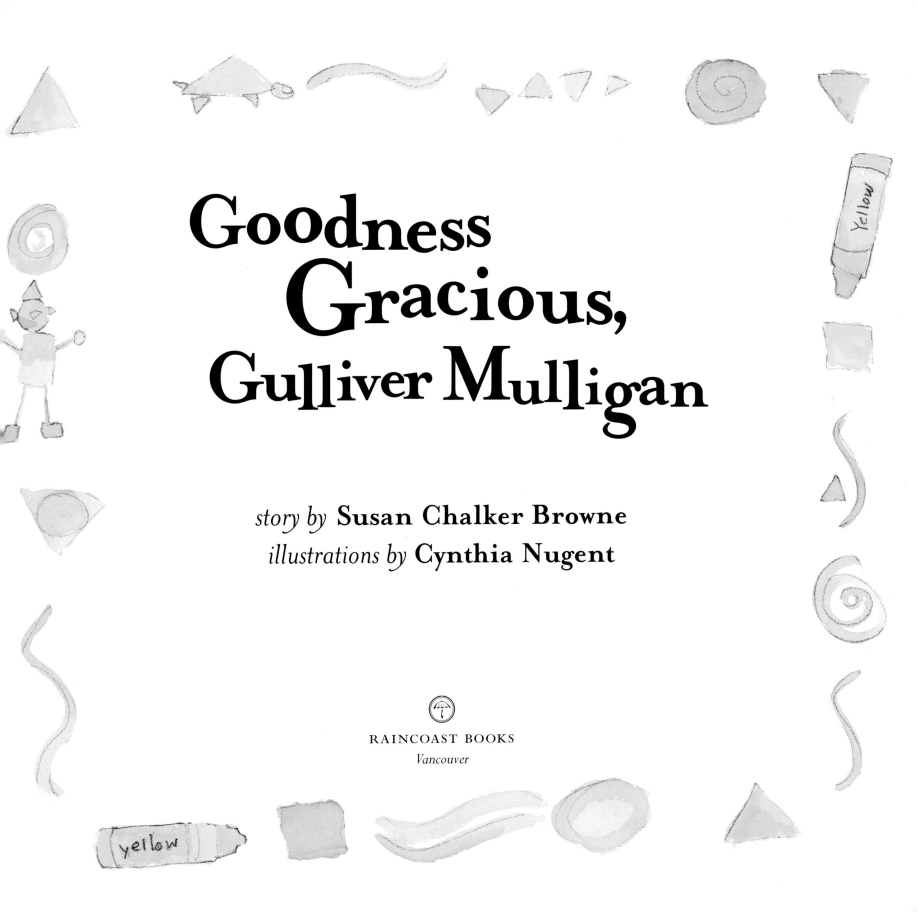

Goodness Gracious, Gulliver Mulligan

story by **Susan Chalker Browne**
illustrations by **Cynthia Nugent**

RAINCOAST BOOKS

Vancouver

For David.
— SCB

For Titus, Heather and Jeremy.
— CN

Gulliver Mulligan stood twice as tall as everyone else in his class. His shoes were size 10, his pants were size 12, and his shirts were size 14. Even his hats were extra large. Gulliver Mulligan was a big boy.

Every afternoon when the children lined up by the door with their backpacks, Gulliver's head hovered over everyone like a big balloon with a face. Mrs. Honeytree would clap her hands together, look way up and say, "Goodness Gracious, Gulliver Mulligan! Never in all my life have I seen such a large child! How wonderful to be so big!"

All the children would stomp down the corridor, out the double doors and into their parents' cars. Mrs. Honeytree would watch them march past, then whisper to Mrs. Coveyduck from Grade 3, "Poor Gulliver Mulligan. Gulliver Mulligan has no friends."

Each morning for breakfast, Gulliver ate three boiled eggs, four slices of toast and five bowls of Rice Krispies. And each morning Gulliver's Mom said, "Gulliver, dear, would you like to ask a friend to play after school?"

Gulliver would bite his thumbnail and stare at his cereal.

"How about Bobby Birdwhistle? He seems like a lovely boy."

Gulliver watched his mother peel another egg. He listened as she asked him questions. And sometimes he would smile. But Gulliver Mulligan never said a word.

Gulliver's Mom would shake her head sadly. "Poor Gulliver," she worried to herself. "Gulliver Mulligan has no friends."

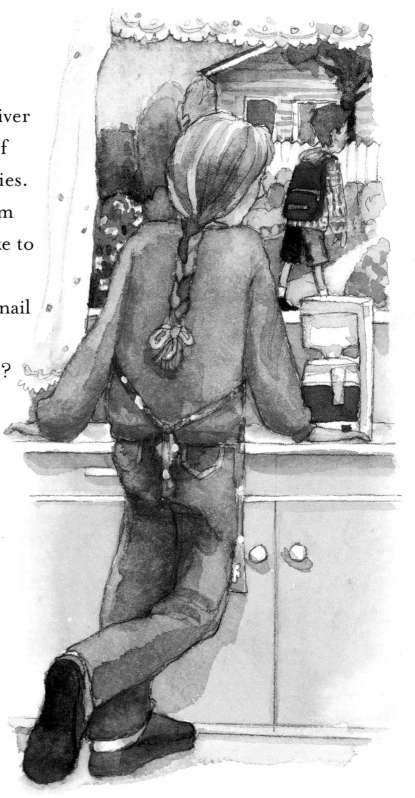

After school when all the children gathered on the street with their bikes and bats, Gulliver Mulligan would sit on the grass and play with his trucks. He watched the children play hide-and-seek. He listened to them laugh and quarrel. And sometimes he would smile. But Gulliver Mulligan never said a word.

On some days a mean girl named Hogarth would come around just to tease. "Gulliver Mulligan is so big ... Gulliver Mulligan is a PIG!" Then she'd throw dogberries in Gulliver's face and run away laughing.

One foggy morning at Gulliver's school all the children were playing inside. Gulliver sat nearby with his crayons and paper. He watched the children dress up in droopy hats and jackets. He listened as their dinky cars roared through the sandbox. And sometimes he would smile. But Gulliver Mulligan never said a word.

Suddenly there was a loud knock on the classroom door. In came the principal, Mrs. Pumpkinhead. She wore a bright orange dress with black triangles and a green collar. "Good morning, class!"

"Good morning, Mrs. Pumpkinhead!"

Beside Mrs. Pumpkinhead stood a very small boy. His stiff yellow hair stood up straight. He wore a pale yellow shirt, brilliant yellow pants and sneakers decorated with smiling yellow suns.

"This is Mortimer Goss," said the principal. Her voice rumbled like a truck. "Mortimer Goss is new in town and now he's in your class. Good day, children."

"Good day, Mrs. Pumpkinhead."

Out went Mrs. Pumpkinhead. Little Mortimer stood alone, shivering like a bowl of Jell-O. Mrs. Honeytree clapped her hands together, looked way down and said, "Goodness Gracious, Mortimer Goss! Never in all my life have I seen such a small child! How wonderful to be so small!" She took his hand. "Sit down here with Gulliver Mulligan. I believe there's just enough room here for a little fellow like you."

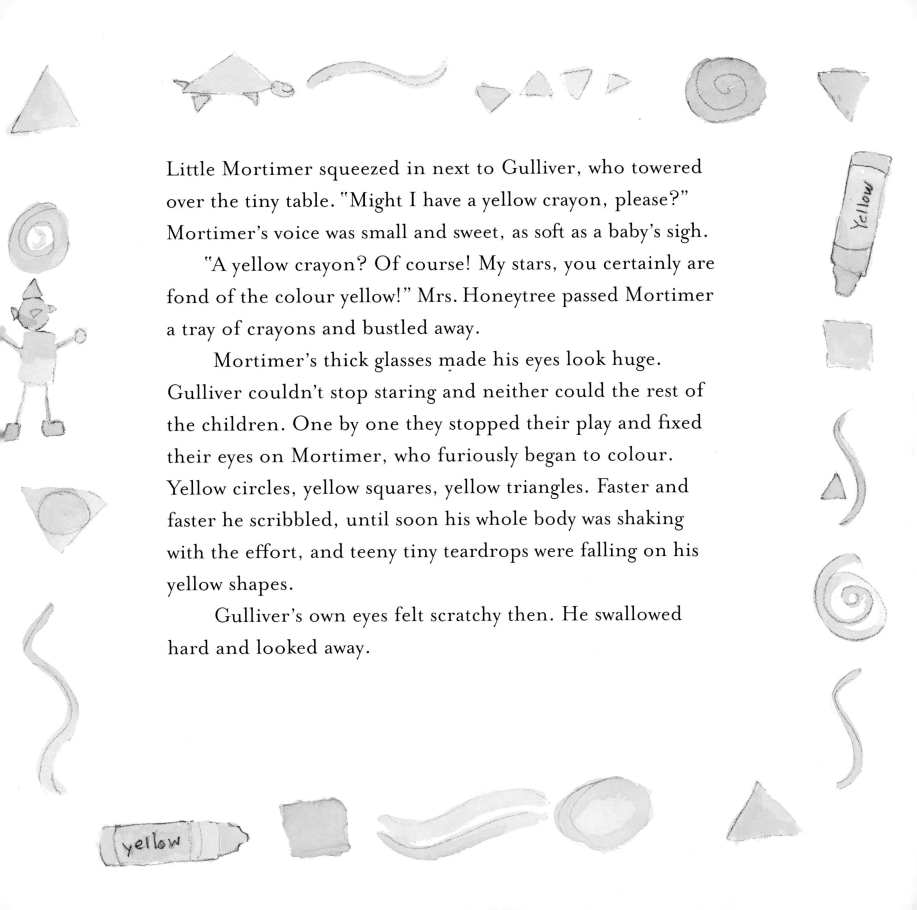

Little Mortimer squeezed in next to Gulliver, who towered over the tiny table. "Might I have a yellow crayon, please?" Mortimer's voice was small and sweet, as soft as a baby's sigh.

"A yellow crayon? Of course! My stars, you certainly are fond of the colour yellow!" Mrs. Honeytree passed Mortimer a tray of crayons and bustled away.

Mortimer's thick glasses made his eyes look huge. Gulliver couldn't stop staring and neither could the rest of the children. One by one they stopped their play and fixed their eyes on Mortimer, who furiously began to colour. Yellow circles, yellow squares, yellow triangles. Faster and faster he scribbled, until soon his whole body was shaking with the effort, and teeny tiny teardrops were falling on his yellow shapes.

Gulliver's own eyes felt scratchy then. He swallowed hard and looked away.

The next day at Gulliver's school there was a nature walk.
"Leaves, children!" said Mrs. Honeytree. "Red, orange and
gold. We'll bring them back and make a beautiful collage
for our wall."

Mrs. Honeytree wore a pink headband and shiny blue
pants. She raced through the woods, plucking leaves right
and left. "Breathe deeply, class," she commanded. "Fresh fall
air stimulates the blood!" Behind her the children huffed and
puffed, scrambled and tripped — especially Mortimer Goss.
But the faster he churned his wee little legs, the further he
fell behind.

Soon the group stopped by Lilypad Pond. "Oh, class,"
cried Mrs. Honeytree. "Look at all the lovely ducks and
swans! My stars, they are chubby. Somebody's bringing them
lots of breadcrumbs."

Suddenly she stared at the children, then clapped her
hand over her mouth. Someone was missing ... Mortimer Goss
was gone!

"Class!" roared Mrs. Honeytree. "Drop everything and line up now! Mortimer's missing and we have to find him!"

The boys and girls lined up quickly.

"Hector and Hugo, check the path for clues. Gertrude and Gladys, check the bushes. Gulliver, you check the trees. And please, this time let's all stay together!"

Back they tramped over the trail. Mrs. Honeytree huffed and puffed, scrambled and tripped, while Gulliver brought up the rear. Soon they heard a small squeak.

"Mortimer?" whispered Mrs. Honeytree.

"Yes," came the squeak. "It's me, Mortimer!"

Mrs. Honeytree crouched down and peered into the thick bushes. Deep inside was a brilliant patch of yellow. "Mortimer? Are you okay?"

"No," wept Mortimer. "I'm not. I'm stuck beneath a big tree trunk."

"Don't worry, Mortimer!" said Mrs. Honeytree. "I'll have that nasty old trunk off you in no time. Everyone stand back!"

A great hush fell over the children like a blanket. They all stepped back ten paces. Mrs. Honeytree rolled up the sleeves of her pale pink sweatshirt and waded into the bushes. A long pointy branch stabbed her in the armpit! Another one stabbed her in the neck! "OUCH! THAT SMARTS!" yelled Mrs. Honeytree as she staggered and steadied herself. Slowly she crouched low like a weightlifter, grunted twice — and disappeared headfirst into the bushes!

"Mrs. Honeytree!" shouted all the children.

A blond head covered with leaves popped up from the bushes. "No problem, class!" gasped Mrs. Honeytree. "I have another idea." Out she stumbled. Her bright pink hairband hung around her neck. Crushed blueberries splattered her sweatshirt. And white underwear winked through the holes in her shiny blue pants. She clutched Gulliver Mulligan by his chequered shirt. "Gulliver, it's all up to you now," she said. "You're the only one big enough to lift that tree! You've got to save Mortimer Goss!"

Slowly, Gulliver nodded. He swallowed hard. "Okay, Mrs. Honeytree," he said, and his poor voice croaked like a frog. "I'll try."

Mrs. Honeytree's jaw dropped.

"Well," she said. "Everyone step way back! Gulliver Mulligan has a job to do!"

A shivery silence descended. Gulliver stepped into the bushes and reached down. He grabbed the tree trunk pinning Mortimer, and yanked hard. The sound of splintering wood shattered the stillness. Bits of bark zinged through the air. Damp earth gushed from the ground like lava. Gulliver raised the tree trunk high over his head …

"Gulliver, stop!" commanded Mrs. Honeytree. Gulliver stopped, the tree trunk shaking in his hands. "Look behind you!" Slowly, Gulliver turned his head. Dangling and kicking from the end of the tree was a red-faced Mortimer Goss!

"Put me down!" shouted Mortimer.

"Oh my stars!" said Mrs. Honeytree.

"Oh dear," mumbled Gulliver Mulligan. Ever so slightly 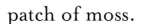 he jiggled his tree and off popped Mortimer onto a spongy patch of moss.

"Mortimer are you hurt?" cried Mrs. Honeytree.

"I don't think so," Mortimer said softly. "Mrs. Honeytree, you were going so fast I had to stop and rest. That's when I looked through these bushes and saw a beautiful yellow flower growing all by itself." He unfolded his small fist. Inside was the most perfect little buttercup.

"Oh, Mortimer! A buttercup in autumn! Whoever heard of such a thing? What a wonderful discovery!" Mrs. Honeytree turned to Gulliver. "Gulliver Mulligan, thank you. Your strength and courage saved Mortimer!"

Gulliver smiled. "You're welcome," he said in his gravelly voice. And all the children jumped and cheered, "Hooray!"

Gulliver Mulligan was the hero of the school. Mrs. Pumpkinhead called an assembly and put a gold medal around his neck. "Gulliver Mulligan," she said, "we're so proud of you."

Gulliver took a deep bow. "Thank you," he whispered hoarsely. Then everyone in the auditorium (including Gulliver's mom!) sprang to their feet in a standing ovation.

Afterwards, Mrs. Honeytree had an enormous ice-cream cake for everyone in the class and Gulliver had the biggest piece. *The Daily News* took a picture of Gulliver and Mortimer and put it on the front page.

The Daily News

WEATHER

Morning — Sun
Afternoon — Tornado
Evening — Mild

Plague of Turtles Hits Schoolyard A25

TV star gets pet kitten B6

HomeTeam Creamed

Sports Final A56

GIANT SAVES BUTTERCUP BOY

Mulligan and Goss with Medal and Buttercup

In an extraordinary act of **childhood** heroism and **strength,** extra-large Gulliver Mulligan saved fellow **student,** Mortimer Goss, from a tree.

"Yellow's my favourite colour," explained Goss when asked about the near-tragic incident in the Lilypad Pond vicinity

Details A6-7

Local boy eats 49 hotdogs for charity C5   Comics and Horoscope D8

From then on, Gulliver Mulligan and Mortimer Goss were always seen together.

"You're my best friend, Gulliver Mulligan," Mortimer would say in his small, sweet voice.

"And you're my best friend too, Mortimer," Gulliver would reply in his gravelly voice as they sat at their tiny table drawing pictures.

"Goodness gracious, what a happy ending!" thought Mrs. Honeytree, who was never allowed another nature walk, not for the rest of her teaching career.

Raincoast Books acknowledges the ongoing financial support of the Government of Canada through
The Canada Council for the Arts and the Book Publishing Industry Development Program (BPIDP);
and the Government of British Columbia through the BC Arts Council.

Edited by Simone Doust
Design by Ingrid Paulson

NATIONAL LIBRARY OF CANADA CATALOGUING IN PUBLICATION DATA
Browne, Susan Chalker, 1958–
    Goodness gracious, Gulliver Mulligan

    ISBN 1-55192-560-5 (bound)   ISBN 1-55192-679-2 (pbk)

    I. Nugent, Cynthia, 1954– II. Title.
PS8553.R691G66 2002   jC813'.6   C2002-910530-7
PZ7.B822155Go 2002

LIBRARY OF CONGRESS CATALOGUE NUMBER: 2002091843

Raincoast Books   *In the United States:*
9050 Shaughnessy Street   Publishers Group West
Vancouver, British Columbia   1700 Fourth Street
Canada   V6P 6E5   Berkeley, California
www.raincoast.com   94710

Printed in Hong Kong, China by Book Art Inc., Toronto
10 9 8 7 6 5 4 3 2